MIDDLE SCHOOL

HOW I GOT LOST IN LONDON

JAMES PATTERSON

MIDDLE SCHOOL

HOW I GOT LOST IN LONDON

Published by Young Arrow, 2014

2 4 6 8 10 9 7 5 3 1

First published in Great Britain in 2014 by
Young Arrow
Random House, 20 Vauxhall Bridge Road,
London SW1V 2SA

www.randomhouse.co.uk

Addresses for companies within The Random House Group Limited can
be found at: www.randomhouse.co.uk/offices.htm

The Random House Group Limited Reg. No. 954009

A CIP catalogue record for this book
is available from the British Library

ISBN 9780099568087
ISBN 9780099596653 (export edition)

The Random House Group Limited supports the Forest Stewardship
Council® (FSC®), the leading international forest-certification
organisation. Our books carrying the FSC label are printed on
FSC®-certified paper. FSC is the only forest-certification scheme
supported by the leading environmental organisations, including
Greenpeace. Our paper procurement policy can be found at
www.randomhouse.co.uk/environment

Printed and bound in Great Britain
by Clays Ltd, St Ives plc

To Philip Yanakov and his mother Victoria who, through their generosity, help get kids reading.

MIDDLE SCHOOL

HOW I GOT LOST
IN LONDON

CHAPTER 1

CHECKLIST

Checklist of things you should bring for a transatlantic flight to London:

1 *Yourself.* Which in my case, is me. More about me in Chapter 2. I mean, there's more about me in the whole book, obviously— I'm the guy on the cover— but Chapter 2 is where we get the introductions out of the way.

> **CHECKLIST**
> ☑ YOURSELF
> ☐ CLOTHES
> ☐ TOOTHPASTE
> ☐ CHECKLIST
> ☐ CHECKLIST of the CHECKLIST
> ☐ CHECKLIST OF the CHECKLIST of the CHECKLIST

Anyway, back to the checklist. On to item two...

2 Er...what else? Oh yes, almost forgot: your clothes, toothpaste, and stuff like that. In other words, the kind of stuff your mom packs for you.

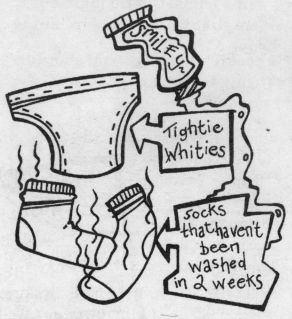

SMILEY

Tightie Whities

socks that haven't been washed in 2 weeks

3 But as this is a checklist, I guess you should really *check* your mom has packed your stuff. Otherwise it wouldn't be much of a checklist.

4 On second thoughts, let's live dangerously.

5 And...that's it, really.

Checklist of things you probably *don't* need on a transatlantic flight to London—but which come in handy anyway:

1 Spaghetti Bolognese.

Yeah? you're thinking.
And? you're thinking.
Spaghetti Bolognese?! you're thinking.
What's that got to do with anything? Well, as my homeroom teacher Mr. Rourke would say, "read on Macduff," which is something to do with Shakespeare. See? You've learned something already!

PRE-TRIP NERVES

So, spaghetti Bolognese. Hold that thought. We'll come back to it. For the time being, all you really need to know is that the transatlantic flight in question involved me—me as in Rafe Khatchadorian, your friendly neighborhood narrator. And if you know me from *Middle School: The Worst Years of My Life* and/or *Middle School: Get Me Out of Here!* then hi, grab a seat, it's good to see you again. I hope you enjoyed the other books, especially the bits about me.

And if you liked the bits with Jeanne "love-of-my-life, but-why-oh-why-won't-she-love-me-back" Galletta, well, the good news is, she's in this story too. Matter of fact, she was also on the transatlantic flight to London.

And if you really hated the bits with Miller the Killer in, 'cause he's such a bully...well, the bad news is he's in this tale too. He was on the transatlantic flight to London as well.

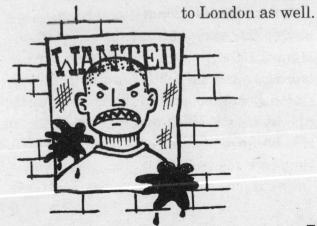

Why? Well, because this story is something that happened during my time at Hills Village Middle School, when I went on a Living History trip to London.

But wait—we're not in London yet. We're not even on the flight yet. Our tale begins one Saturday morning in the deserted parking lot of Hills Village school. Deserted apart from a coach about to take us to the airport, and ten kids with backpacks on, moms and dads fussing round them. And teachers saying things like, "Don't worry, Mrs. Abbott, everything is taken care of. Jason will be fine." And, "Yes, Mr. Swann. Our insurance is fully up to date—there's absolutely nothing to worry about."

That was Ms. Donatello, who despite having the name of a Teenage Mutant Ninja Turtle isn't green, definitely isn't a teenager, and no way is a ninja (although she may well be a mutant. Who knows?). She teaches English and was along for the ride because she'd always wanted to visit England.

Mr. Rourke was there too, and Mr. Dwight the principal. They all had this weird out-of-school look about them. At first I couldn't work out what it was, but then it clicked: They were all smiling. They all looked happy.

Mom couldn't stay, not like the other parents. No fussing for me. My sister Georgia had a piano lesson. So Mom dropped me off, straightened my collar, gave me a kiss on the forehead, and told me to be good. And that was it. Off she went. I watched the family SUV turn out of the lot and head back into town. The

last thing I saw was Georgia.
Or, to be precise, the back of
Georgia's head.

And all of a sudden I felt real lonely.
Even though I was surrounded by other
kids—kids I went to school with, whose
fart smells and body odor I knew as well
as my own. Even with Jeanne Galletta
there, and Miller the Killer there, and
Dylan Stephenson, and Sasha Smallbones
and all the rest...

...even with all those guys there, what
I felt as I watched Mom and Georgia drive
away was lonely. Like I was already miles
away from home.

Lucky I had Leonardo the Silent with
me.

CHAPTER 3

LOTS OF AMPHIBIOUS CREATURES IN THIS BIT

Leonardo the Silent. It's him who draws the pictures. And he's my best friend. See, I'm not exactly what you'd call popular at school. There's a reason I stood at the assembly point feeling lonely. It wasn't just because I was staring at the exhaust pipe of Mom's SUV. It's because, well…I don't have many friends. Or really, to be precise again, *any* friends.

But here's a secret.

Ready?

[Clears throat. Looks left and right. Leans in close to whisper.]

Leonardo the Silent isn't real.

Well, I mean, he's *real*—in the sense that he's a *real* imaginary friend. And he's a real *good* imaginary friend too. (See what I did there?) Just that he's not "real." He doesn't have skin and blood and arms and a backside.

He's my twin brother who died, when I was so young I never even got to be sad about it, and now I keep him around as what you might call a "special friend." He's a good special friend. Never lets me down.

Okay, *rarely* lets me down.

And he always tells it like it is. What's more, he's the other person in my life with a name like a Teenage Mutant Ninja Turtle. He's not green, he's not yet a teenager, and he's not a mutant...

...but when it comes to drawing, he's a ninja.

And if it wasn't for art, and for Leo...
well, things would be different for me, I
guess. I'd find it hard: the problems I have
with my classmates, with my teachers,
with rules, with reality. I'd find it even
harder than I already do.

Anyway, back to the parking lot, back
to that assembly. Here's where the story
really began, and in the most innocent and
unexpected of ways. A way you could never
predict in a million years. It began with a
roll-call.

Trust me on this: If you go on a school
trip—and especially if you go on a school
trip to a foreign country—you have to put
up with a lot of roll-calls. You get to say
"Here" a lot. Just one word. "Here." Hardly
the Gettysburg Address. Not exactly a
Shakespearean speech. And in the privacy
of my bedroom I could say the word "here"
a thousand times in a row and nothing
untoward would happen.

But the one time I had to say it in front
of the rest of the trip. *The one time.* Oh,
and the first time as well.

It sounded like a frog burping. No. A frog with hiccups burping. A frog with hiccups burping while it's being strangled by another frog fed up with the first frog's endless hiccupping.

That, really, was the beginning of all my problems. Like if I'd managed to say "Here" right that first time, then maybe none of what happened would have happened.

CHAPTER 4

A ROLL-CALL OF ROLL-CALLS

Roll-call at the airport.

Miller the Killer got a big laugh with his impression of my "Here." His sounded like a witch. Mine had sounded like a hiccupping, burping strangled frog but his sounded like a witch. What I'm trying to say is that even though his didn't even sound like mine, he still got a laugh.

I actually broke out in a sweat when it came to my turn to say "Here" for the second time that day. But I struggled through with no major limbs lost. It wasn't great but at least it only got suppressed giggles—rather than the unrestrained guffawing that had accompanied my first one.

Roll-call on the plane.

Miller the Killer was doing his bit for the environment by recycling the same joke.

My own "Here"? A masterclass in the art. An Oscar-worthy "Here." But it was too late: The damage had been done at first assembly.

Why, oh why couldn't someone invent a time machine, so I could go back and do it again?

The next disaster came when we took our seats on the plane and Miller the Killer ended up next to Jeanne Galletta. Not only that, but he was completely wasting the opportunity.

He wasn't even talking to her!

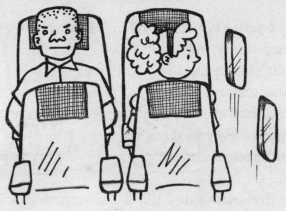

I mean, if I'd been sitting next to her…

…well, I probably wouldn't have been talking to her either. But that's not the point. The point was, he was sitting next to Jeanne and I was sitting next to Ms. Donatello. Meaning any chance of a sneaky peak at an R-rated movie was dashed for the whole of the nine-hour flight. Great.

Was there no justice?

Was Justice having the day off?

To make matters *even* worse, I then sat down but forgot to take off my backpack. And to try and save face, I pretended I'd deliberately sat down with my backpack on—even though my nose was virtually touching the seat in front and my spine was about to snap.

I probably would have stayed that way but a stewardess insisted I remove my backpack. So I curled  my lip and sighed like I thought she was denying me my civil rights—when in fact I wanted to hug her for sparing me the torture of wearing my backpack all the way to London.

And that was it. I sat and fumed. And while everyone else got excited about watching horror movies, I had nine hours of heroic-duck films to look forward to. *Gah!*

As we took off, and the journey began, I noticed two things: (a) that Miller the Killer was looking a mite green about the gills and (b) that lunch was being served. And it was spaghetti Bolognese.

"Are you thinking what I'm thinking?" whispered Leo.

I was.

CHAPTER 5

THE BOLOGNESE BIT—PART 1

Justice may well have been having the day off, but Luck was by my side, because Donatello had fallen asleep. Her head was back, her mouth slightly open, and she was making a strange humming sound, like a wine taster on TV.

hmmmm

Across the aisle Miller the Killer sat beside Jeanne. By now he was sitting stock still with his eyes kind of bugging out of his head, and he hadn't touched his food. The pleasures of vacuum-packed airline spaghetti Bolognese were lost to him.

In fact, forget about lunch—Miller looked like he was having trouble keeping his breakfast down.

I'd like to say it was all Leo's idea, what happened next.

So I will.

It was all Leo's idea what happened next.

In the pocket of the seat in front of me was a magazine full of fascinating features about beaches and hotel rooms. There was a card showing how to inflate your life jacket and a magazine full of duty-free products.

These things were of zero interest to me.

What I wanted was the other thing in the pocket. The bag you're supposed to grab if you're feeling like you want to hurl. The sick bag.

You know that bit in *Mission: Impossible*, where Tom Cruise kind of abseils into the secure room? Where he

needs to steal the data without
setting off the alarms? Where
he's sweating and stuff, and he...

Okay, you know the bit.

That's how careful I was as I removed
the sick bag from the pocket then turned
away slightly so Miller the Killer wouldn't
see me. (Not that he
was likely to be
watching anyway,
because he was still
doing the eye-bugging
thing and staring at
the seat in front of
him.) Then I poured
my Bolognese into it.

Correction: I poured Donatello's Bolognese into it. But she wasn't going to mind. Judging by the *yum-yum* sounds she was making, she was enjoying a scrumptious meal in her sleep.

Then I took a spoon from my lunch plate and called across the aisle: "Hey, *Miller*!" And when he turned his head to look at me, I dipped the spoon into the sick bag and started to eat the Bolognese.

CHAPTER 6

THE BOLOGNESE BIT—PART 2

There's something called a *chain reaction*. It's where one action causes a reaction, and that in turn causes another reaction, and so on and so on (and so on). It's a science thing. And we're talking about what happened on a Living History trip—which is humanities, but what the heck. It's all learning, right?

So LISTEN UP, class! Today we're going to learn all about chain reactions.

It begins with Miller the Killer turning his head to see me eating Bolognese from the sick bag. Only he thinks I'm eating...

Too much information? Too much information. You get the picture.

...So anyway. I munched.

I chewed.

I did a bit of slurping too.

I even wiped Bolognese from my chin. And—inspired by Ms. Donatello—I made a whole lot of *yum-yum* noises.

Hey Miller! Hmmm Yummy!

I mean, I *really* yummed it up.

And Miller turned greener and greener. The muscles in his face and neck began to twitch. His chest started to heave like there was an alien creature inside him.

"Yum-yum!" I said.

His cheeks bulged.

His head pecked forward.

He clamped a hand over his mouth.

"Delicious!" I said.

And then Miller heaved and barfed. Puke spurted through his fingers. Beside him Jeanne Galletta shouted, "EWW!" and tried to get away. But it was too late, because Miller the Killer was unleashing a full-on gusher.

A chunderstorm.

A hurlicane.

A barfquake registering one hundred on the sick-ter scale.

And unlike me he didn't have a sick bag. Instead, he just kept his hand clamped over his mouth. But it couldn't contain the fountain of cookie-toss that was forced through his fingers.

His hand acted like a shower head and the vomit sprayed far and wide. It went all over Jeanne next to him and all over the kids who sat in the seats in front. And—in a way—it went all over everyone around him. Because even though it didn't *physically* touch everyone…that's when the chain reaction began.

Barf!

Hurl!

Bleck!

Rurk!

A tsunami of spew.

A tsunami is a big wave, right? And what do waves do but roll right over you. *Engulf* you.

"You," in this case, being all of the passengers in the section. "All of the passengers in the section," in this case, being the members of the Hills Village Living History trip to London.

Pretty much all of them lost their lunch.

Yes, I think I'm right in saying that with the exception of the teachers (who must need strong stomachs to work at Hills Village anyway—probably an essential qualification for the job), all the kids blew chunks.

Some made it into sick bags. Some didn't.

And we were on a plane. You can't just open the windows and let the smell out. It circulates. It hangs in the air. And, I'm telling you, there isn't an air-filtration system in the world that can deal with the combined spew-smell of ten puking kids.

It was a loooong flight.

CHAPTER 7

"NURSE, THE SCREENS. WE'RE GOING TO HAVE TO OPERATE"

You'd have figured that zero friends means none to lose.

If, for example, you were the one responsible for beginning a chunder chain that turned a nine-hour transatlantic flight into a living nightmare, then at least you couldn't be less popular than you already were. Right?

Wrong.

It turns out you *can* be even less popular than you were. Take my classmates. Not only did they hate me for

beginning the chunder-fest, but they hated
me because I'd riled Miller.

Miller's a bit like a big dog—ugly,
vicious, but as long as you did nothing to
upset him, you had nothing to fear.

But I had done something to upset him.
And he wasn't going to take it out just on
me. *Oohh no.*

"Better get out of my way, turdbreath."
SNARL!

"I've got a Chinese burn with your
name on it, snot-for-brains." *BARK!*

He was going to take it out on the rest
of the trip too.

You ever hear the expression *persona
non grata*? Meaning when nobody will talk

to you? That was me. Imagine the pecking order of pain: Miller the Killer at the top. My classmates in the middle. Every single one of them looking down on me...right at the bottom.

So. A mission—Operation: Popularity. I'll be the first to admit it wasn't much of a title, but it wasn't designed to win awards. It was designed to return me to the good books of my fellow Living History trippers. Or at least get me out of their bad ones.

Now to come up with some half-decent ideas for the operation.

Some half-decent ideas for Operation: Popularity:

ONE. Banana-eating contest
You know how we always get bananas in our lunch, right? And you know how the bananas get all soft and sweaty and nobody wants to eat them? So my idea was: Start a banana-eating contest with all the unwanted bananas.

GOOD POiNTS: It would be *hilarious*. Food-eating contests are always funny and the sight of me eating banana after banana would bring the house down.

BAD POiNTS: A possible repeat of the chunderstorm on the flight over. Okay, let's face it—an almost *inevitable* repeat of the chunderstorm on the flight over.

TWO. Being kind and generous to all my classmates

GOOD POiNTS: Not only would I make friends—I'd make proper friends. Lasting friends. I'd have friends.

BAD POiNTS: It would take a loooong time. This is like one of those long-term plans. I mean, if I was going to try to make myself popular by being kind and generous, then I really needed to start doing that in the first grade.

THRee. Save them from the merciless taunting and bullying of Miller the Killer

GOOD POiNTS: *Bingo!* We have a winner! All I have to do is stop Miller's merciless taunting and bullying and for the rest of my London trip I'd be treated like a god. It's a great idea! Why didn't I think of it before?

BAD POINTS:

I have no idea how to stop the merciless taunting and bullying of Miller the Killer. Okay, that suggestion has to go on ice. If that suggestion calls, put it on hold.

I have a suggestion

FOUR. Make a full and frank apology

GOOD POINTS: It's what they do on TV! It's what the President would do (if the President had eaten Bolognese out of a sick bag and caused the Vice-President to barf).

BAD POiNTS: I'd have to make a full and frank apology. The thing about a full and frank apology is…Wait a minute—how the heck do you make a full and frank apology?

Okay. Hold those thoughts. For the time being, let's start with a **Popularity Score: 0.**

Zero. Nada.

Squat.

Aim: To raise that dismal Popularity Score.

We landed. We disembarked our puke-smelling plane. That's what you do, by the way. You don't "get off" a plane. You *disembark* it. We assembled. There was a roll-call.

"Here!"

Not as good as my Oscar-winning "Here," but nowhere near the calamity of my disastrous first attempt.

After roll-call we marched through Heathrow Airport and trooped onto a coach. The coach was big enough for a whole two seats each. Which was good, because it meant I definitely didn't have to sit next to Miller. But it was also bad, because it meant I didn't have an excuse to sit next to Jeanne Galletta. And I needed an excuse to sit next to her.

Instead, I settled into the seat behind her. There was a roll-call. I was about to open my mouth for my latest rendition when I heard Miller pipe up instead.

"Here," he said, his lame impression rearing its ugly head again.

There were titters from around the bus.

Great, I thought. *This is a joke that travels. And now Miller's got his feet back on the ground—now he's stopped either puking or worrying about puking—he's decided to resurrect it. That's just PEACHY.*

Still, I was thankful for small mercies. At least he wasn't sitting nearby. He'd elbowed his way on and claimed the whole of the backseat as his own. From there he could launch attacks on the earlobes of anyone unlucky enough to be sitting nearby.

For a while, all we heard as the coach moved out of the Heathrow parking lot was the sound of ears being flicked.

I looked out of the window. *Hey! We're driving on the wrong side of the road. HEY, MR. DRIVER! Patrick* (that was his name)—*we're driving on the...*

"They drive on a different side of the road in England, doofus," whispered Leo the Silent, sparing me any new embarrassment.

Popularity Score: (still) 0.

CHAPTER 8

SMELLY NAPPIES VS DIRTY DIAPERS

Here's a bunch of stuff I noticed is different in England:

1 People drive on the wrong side of the road. (Thanks to Leo for pointing that one out.)

2 The light switches: English light switches are kind of little and weird.

3 The toilets: If you lift the lid of a toilet in England there's hardly any water in it. (Go figure.)

4 When they boil water, they don't use a stove like at home. They do it in a "kettle."

5 They use the kettle to make a drink called tea, which they drink a lot. And they make a dumb face when they drink the tea, like "Aaahhh..." Like this drink that actually looks like

puddle-water is the most delicious
thing in the world.

Aaaaah!

6 They don't have drive-through ATMs.
(I know!)
7 It's kind of crowded everywhere, and
they have queues and stuff.
8 They have this spread called Marmite.
It's *disgusting*. It looks like tar and
smells like meat. They spread it on
their toast to
eat with
their tea.

PEE-UUU!

C'mon,
stick your
nose a
little closer

MARMITE

9 They have weird numbering systems for the floors in their hotels. So when you get into the elevator—which in England is called a "lift"—and you try to get to your floor…Chaos.

so...these must be?
second floor
first floor
ground floor

10 Pants in England are what you wear *under* your pants. What we call shorts, they call pants. Oh, and they call closets "cupboards." They call trucks "lorries." They call flashlights "torches." They call diapers "nappies."

WHAT?

11 When they need to call the emergency services they don't call 911—they call 999.

And that last one. Number 11. That's an important one. You'll be hearing more about that later. Oh, and number 9? More about that is coming right about...

...now.

CHAPTER 9

THE BIT WITH NUMBER 9 IN IT

Anyway. Like I said, Miller was on the backseat, master of his domain—an evil king ruling over the rear of the bus, as far away from the teachers as he could manage. And there he set about terrorizing anyone within flicking distance. As the bus set off, all we could hear was the sound of earlobes being flicked.

Flick.

"Oww!"

Flick.

"OWW!"

Each one made me more unpopular. I mean, it wasn't like anyone had actually ragged on *Miller* for starting the puke chain. Who would dare? But you know how in war they have such a thing as a pre-emptive strike? When one side launches missiles before the other?

That was what Miller was doing.

Flick.

"OUCH!"

Pre-emptive strike on Sasha Smallbones.

Flick.

"Oww!"

Really vicious pre-emptive strike on Philip Yanakov.

All my fault.

Something needed to be done.

And so, as we drove down the freeway (or "motorway" as they call it in England), I shuffled forward in my seat.

"Jeanne," I said between the seats, "I need to tell you something. I need your help."

She ignored me. Just stared straight ahead.

I plowed on regardless. "I wanted to say sorry about what happened on the plane. I want to explain myself. See, Miller was ragging on me and…" (Wow, nearly made a big mistake then. Nearly went on to admit that I'd been jealous he sat next to her.) "…and I know he was only doing it because I said that weird 'Here' at the first roll-call. And, as a matter of fact, he's still doing it. Did you hear him? Did you HEAR him?! *Twice*. Twice since we landed. But anyway, I guess I deserve it now. But my *point* is: I didn't deserve it *then*. I mean, maybe a bit, because my 'Here' wasn't exactly the best 'Here,' I'd be the first to admit it. But I just thought—and I still feel—that Miller's ragging was too much. How do you say it? What's the word again? *Disproportionate*. And I wanted to teach him a lesson, which is why I came up with the idea of eating the Bolognese out of the sick bag. And if I wasn't such a doofus I would have realized what was going to happen: chain reaction. And now Miller's ragging on everyone just out of pure meanness. Because he's like, well, *mean*. And listen, well…I just wanted to say sorry. First to you and then to everyone else. So this is me saying sorry. And I'm hoping you'll accept my apology and maybe help me apologize to the rest of the trip. Perhaps even tell them yourself. You know, kind of spread it around how sorry I am. Or get an idea of how easy or hard it would be."

It was one of my longest-ever speeches. It was the hardest, most heartfelt thing I think I've said. Leo the Silent applauded by my side.

Shame she was listening to her iPod the whole time. Didn't hear a word I said.

We arrived at our hotel—the Mercury Lodge—checked in, and went to our rooms. Guess who made a mess of getting to their room?

That would be me.

Remember number 9? I used the elevator (I beg your pardon, the "lift") and instead of going up to my floor, managed to go to the floor below.

They liked that, everyone did. They all thought that was *real* funny. Especially You-Know-Who. He was still laughing when I got to the room I was going to be sharing with him.

That's right: I was sharing with Miller. *Could this trip get any worse?*

CHAPTER 10

DEAR EARLOBES, REALLY SORRY ABOUT THIS CHAPTER. LOVE, RAFE XOX

So that was it. The heartfelt-apology option had failed. Which left the, um…other options. Which of those was it going to be? Justice had the day off, remember? Luck had now packed its bags for a week away.

Fate, however, was still with me. And the thing is, I have a good relationship with Fate. Fate has a habit of intervening in the life of Rafe Khatchadorian. And it was about to intervene again…

It happened the next morning.

First stop on our itinerary was Tower Bridge. If you get to Tower Bridge at the right time you get to see it open.

And we were very nearly late because I got the floors on the lift-elevator-whatever-you-call-it wrong again. So by the time I arrived at the bus, Ms. Donatello and Co. were looking furious and Patrick the driver was tapping his watch.

"RAFE KHATCHADORIAN!" yelled Donatello. She shot lasers out of her eyes and I burned to a crisp there and then in the Mercury Lodge Hotel parking lot.

Everyone on the trip gave her a round of applause in gratitude.

Popularity Score: -11.

I boarded the bus, feeling all hot and flustered. The only spare double seat left was at the back. Right in range of Miller, who sat there like royalty. The Earl of Earlobe-Flicking. The Flick King.

Flick.

"OWW!"

That was me that time. Sasha Smallbones, you're in the clear.

Flick.

"OUCH!"

the FLICK King!

Me again. Philip Yanakov's earlobes had the day off.

Flick.
"OWW!"
Yup—me again...

CHAPTER 11

GOING SOFT IN MY YOUNG AGE

We watched Tower Bridge open then close. After that we turned to walk back along the bank of the Thames, dodging jugglers, dog-walkers, people late for work. All of them, well...*English*, and therefore fascinating, like we expected to bump into James Bond at any second. Matter of fact, wasn't that the MI6 headquarters we could see in the distance? The one that explodes in the film?

Bond...
James Bond

Khatchadorian...
Rafe
Khatchadorian

I gazed at a line of sidewalk artists. Some were drawing scenes on paper taped to the sidewalk. Others were inviting passers-by to sit for caricatures.

Farther along we could see the London Eye.

"Hey, Miller," I said. My earlobes were still smarting.

(Big mistake coming up. Wait for it. Big mistake.)

"What you want, Khatchadoofius?" he glowered. Miller always glowers. Unless directed otherwise, assume Miller is glowering.

"Just wondering if you might like to go up on the London Eye?" I said.

(*Thinking how green and sick and ill you looked back there on the plane, buddy.* Just remembering that. Just *relishing* that particular memory...)

He stuck his big ugly face up close to mine. "How about you wonder what the water in the river tastes like, when I throw you in if you don't zip it?"

Oh, wooh! Snappy comeback, is what I think. Self-preservation stops me from saying it, though. Instead, I look at the river and imagine Miller throwing me in. There are things floating in it. The shed skin of sea monsters. Barrels of toxic waste. Alien cartilage. I'm pretty sure I don't want to go in.

So the result of that particular exchange was that I reminded Miller of his phobia. And like a vicious, rabid dog awakened from sleep, he remembered he had to start persecuting me again. My earlobes began throbbing as though anticipating the trauma ahead.

We visited a big warship, the HMS *Belfast*. You know what? There are times it's handy being unpopular. You can walk round battleships alone and let your imagination run free. You don't have to think up lame wisecracks to look cool in front of your friends. Away from the rest of the group I did just that—I let my imagination run free. I could picture sailors at war, hear the crash of machine-gun fire, the screech of a torpedo strike. It felt like being in a movic. For the first timc, I really *got* why we were here.

CHAPTER 12

GiRAFFeS, FAMOUS PEOPLE—iT'S ALL GOiNG ON iN CHAPTeR 12

I've given you a break from My Roll-Call Nightmare but it's the same as Miller and his glowering: Unless I tell you otherwise, just assume we had a roll-call.

By now Miller was saying my "Here" for me. And everyone was yukking it up. Him most of all, but all the other kids too. And I even caught Mr. Dwight smiling. I wasn't even bothering to say "Here" anymore. What was the point? My arch-enemy was doing it for me.

After the HMS *Belfast* we visited a replica of Francis Drake's *Golden Hind*.

Then we made our way
to the Tate Modern—a
huge, cool art gallery,
with a giant pink giraffe
standing on a piece
of grass out front. We
joined other sightseers
to have our lunch,
right by the
legs of the
pink giraffe.

We all had bananas in our packs. Like
I'd predicted, nobody wanted their soft,
warm banana.

"Should I try the banana-
eating competition?" I
whispered to Leo the Silent.
I sat by myself with my
backpack on, nursing my **-11**
Popularity Score.

"Uh-uh," warned Leo.

I thought about ignoring him. I imagined a scene in which I eat everyone's bananas, one after the other. My classmates are delighted. My Popularity Score climbs into double figures. But then...disaster strikes! When we move on I feel my stomach churning and the next second I'm regurgitating banana all over the pink giraffe. I get called Rafe Barf-Giraffe for the rest of the trip and my Popularity Score falls back into minus double figures.

So I took Leo's advice. There would be no banana-eating competition. Not on my watch.

Next, we made our way farther up the bank, past the National Theatre, headed for the big event of the day—a tour around Madame Fifi's House of Wax. Now, it should go without saying that even though we were pretty excited about seeing the main exhibit—Will and Kate! David Beckham! Rihanna!—we were *really* excited about the basement. Because in the basement was Madame Fifi's Temple of

Terrors, where you could see beheadings, guys on spikes, people on the rack, guillotines…

In other words, the gory stuff.

Yeah, yeah, we saw the celebrities. But honestly? Do you really want to stand cycball to cycball with Tom Cruise?

You do?!

Not me. I wanted stuff from out of my world. So I found myself hanging around longest at Henry VIII (he married six times and beheaded two of his wives!), Winston Churchill (he said "We shall never surrender" to Adolf Hitler!), Charles Darwin (it's thanks to him we know monkeys are our ancestors!), Guy Fawkes (he tried to blow up Parliament…Wait: Are we supposed to like him or not?).

Our tour guide was a guy called Gordon. Either he didn't know that everyone was goofing off behind him or he didn't care. Or maybe he had an ace up his sleeve. Maybe he knew the smirking would stop as soon as we went down into the basement. When we got to the Temple of Terrors.

CHAPTER 13

DOWN INTO THE DEPTHS

I was kind of sad to leave the upper floors. And also kind of…

"Scared…?" whispered Leo.

"No, of course I'm not scared," I said.

"Frightened?"

"Frightened is the same as scared," I told him. "And no, I'm not frightened."

"Browning your britches?" he asked.

"You're just using different words to say the same thing. No, I am *not* browning my britches."

I'll let you into a secret: I *was* kind of nervous.

Woah! I don't mean the whole hog. Not like when Georgia freaked out at a not-that-scary episode of *Scooby Doo*. Just a bit crawling-in-the-pit-of-my-stomach nervous. You know the kind. Like you get when you don't know what to expect. When your imagination has taken the words *guillotine*, *beheading*, *gallows*, and *serial killer* and started to run with them.

"Is everyone ready?" asked Gordon, the tour guide. Before, he'd been a bit glass-eyed, like a robot delivering a pre-recorded speech. Now there was no mistaking the glint in his gaze.

"Yeah," we all replied, pretending like we weren't impressed.

Mindful of my Popularity Score (currently: **-11**), I'd decided I was going to be fearless when it came to the Temple of Terrors, so my "Yeah" was the loudest.

"YEAH!"

"Right, then, let's go," said Gordon. He went to open the door but stopped, looking like he'd just remembered something important.

"There's nobody in the group who suffers from a weak heart?" he asked.

"*No*," we replied.

"*NO!*" came my voice, the loudest.

"And everyone knows about the haunting?"

"YEAH!" I shouted, enjoying myself. Really getting into the part.

Oh. I realized I was the only one who'd replied.

Everyone looked at me. Including Gordon, who arched an eyebrow.

"What is your name, young man?" he asked.

"Rafe," I said with a pipsqueak voice.

"And you know about the haunting, do you, Rafe?"

I swallowed. "Yes," I said in an even smaller voice.

"You read about it on the Madame Fifi's website, did you?" he asked, with a strange smile.

"Yes, sir," I replied.

The whole trip was staring at me. Everyone had been dying to hear about the haunting. They weren't sitting down, but if they had been sitting down they would have been on the edge of their seats waiting for the scary story of the Temple of Terrors haunting...

Only for the whole thing to be spoiled by me.

"Excellent," said Gordon. He clapped his hands. "Then without further ado, let us proceed."

He opened the door to reveal winding stone steps that led down into darkness. Everyone else glared at me. All except for Miller, that was. He just glowered as usual.

My Popularity Score took another dip.

Current Popularity Score: -22

Down we went. Down into the depths of Madame Fifi's. It was so much darker than it had been on the upper floors.

At the bottom we heard a rumbling sound. One of the girls gasped but Gordon assured her it was just a passing London Underground train.

(Okay, I admit—it wasn't "one of the girls" who gasped, it was me. Like I say, it was dark, and when I gasp I sound like a girl anyway.)

Wax figures seemed to loom at us from the gloom.

"Cool," we said as we peered at heads on spikes, victims on racks, murderers caught in the act. Really gross, scary stuff. And not just really gross, scary stuff, but really gross, scary stuff that had *actually happened*.

All I'll say about a guy called Vlad the Impaler is that the clue is in the name. And as for Countess Bathory—guess what she figured would be good for her skin? That's right: blood. She actually kidnapped girls and…took a bath…in their…

Too much information?

Sure. Too much information.

"Cool," we said. And yes, I know it doesn't sound like we were taking the whole real-people-dying-gruesome-deaths thing all that seriously, but listen: They died their gruesome deaths a really long time ago. Which makes all the difference. Which means you can say "Cool" without feeling too guilty about it.

"Now, Rafe..." said Gordon. We stopped near a scene of a woman being put to death by seventeenth-century witchfinders.

"Here," I said, out of habit.

"Since you know all about the ghost of Madame Fifi's, I expect you can tell us all about the famous Temple of Terrors wager?"

NO WAY was I going to spoil this one for the rest of class. I shook my head "no" furiously.

Gordon smiled. "Well, I'll tell you then, shall I?"

CHAPTER 14

A NINETEENTH-CENTURY TALE OF DERRING-DO

Over a hundred years ago, two rather well-dressed Victorian gentlemen are taking a tour around the famous Madame Fifi's House of Wax. With them is a lady in whom they both have a romantic interest.

"I say," says one, twirling his mustache, "have you been down to this Temple of Terrors they've been writing about in the *Pall Mall Gazette*? They do say it's frightfully frightful."

"Frightfully frightful indeed," says the second gent, as he adjusts his waistcoat on his ample stomach.

Eleanor (the lady) clutches her pearls. "Oh, Cedric, it sounds perfectly dreadful."

Sensing their chance to impress their lady friend, both men preen.

"A lot of sensationalist rot, no doubt," says William. "The ravings of a journalist with an overactive imagination."

"You don't sound terribly convinced, William," says Eleanor.

"Oh, indeed not, Eleanor, indeed not."

"Well, William," says Cedric, "what say you we descend the steps to discover for ourselves just how frightening this place is?"

"What a wheeze it will be."

And the two gents take the stone steps down into the Temple of Terrors.

"Well, I *say*!" says William. He peers around into the gloom, seeing the grotesque, waxy figures staring sightlessly back at him. His skin crawls with fear. "It's not at all frightening, what?"

"No, not at all frightening," says Cedric, swallowing hard and finding he has a sudden need to use the bathroom.

"Why, I would quite happily spend the night here," says William. Who would quite happily do anything *but* spend the night there.

"And I would quite happily join you," agrees Cedric. Who would rather eat a bowl of rancid horse manure than spend the night in the Temple of Terrors.

"Then how about a friendly wager?" suggests William. Who happens to know his friend has little spare money, and will be unlikely to take him up on the bet.

"What a *splendid* idea," says Cedric, who unbeknownst to William has recently inherited a goodly sum from a favorite aunt.

And so, because both men are more frightened of losing face than they are of the Temple of Terrors, and because both men are so terribly determined to impress the fair Eleanor, they both agree to spend the night...

CHAPTER 15

THE TERRIBLE RETURN OF WILLIAM'S WAGER...

"**N**either man was able to stay the whole night," continued Gordon, as he told the tale. "They ran screaming, wide-eyed with terror, frothing with fear, gibbering about ghosts and horrors. And the very next day, both men were found at their homes…"

Gordon fixed us with a stare. You could have heard a pin drop.

"…*dead*…"

As one, we gasped.

"Both having taken their own lives."

He mimed a noose and stuck out his tongue. "Rerk!"

We gasped again. The wax figures now seemed to crowd in on us. The low light reflected from the pale, gleaming skin of executioners and their victims. The unseeing eyes of murderers seemed to stare at us.

"And so William's Wager remains uncollected," Gordon said, "until the day someone brave enough to dare spend the night in the Temple of Terrors should accept the challenge…"

And with that, he moved on, wearing an air of quiet triumph. We followed meekly behind him, lost for wisecracks.

I felt an elbow in my ribs.

"I bet you're too chicken to take up the wager," whisper-sneered Miller, loud enough for Jeanne to hear.

BA-GAWK!

"I'm not scared of a few wax models," I whisper-sneered right back.

"Bet y'are…"

"Bet I'm not," I said.

"Bet you're too chicken to accept William's Wager," Miller said again.

"Bet I'm *not*."

Over a century since William and Cedric had pretended they weren't scared, me and Miller were doing the same. But

William and Cedric were guys in the past, right? People were dumb then. They didn't have TiVO or CGI or YouTube. It would be different with me and Miller, right?

Wrong.

Before I knew it, Miller and I were daring each other back and forth. And word had spread through the group. I sensed a chance—my big chance—to improve my Popularity Score and impress Jeanne and get one over on Miller—all at the same time.

I could win.

For once, I could win.

"Yeah," I said, "I accept the wager. Just as long as you do too."

"It's a deal," Miller said with a grin on his face.

He hadn't batted an eyelid. Wasn't fazed at all. Just accepted the bet. Which meant he was thinking exactly what I was thinking. And what I was thinking was this:

No way were we really going to spend the night in the Temple of Terrors. As soon as the teachers had a roll-call and discovered us missing they'd return to Madame Fifi's and fetch us. Oh, sure, we were going to be in a truckload of trouble with Donatello and Dwight. But look at the positives: the increased Popularity Score, the admiration of Jeanne...The fact that I would get all this without actually having to spend the night in the Temple of Terrors. It was the best idea I'd had all trip.

Wasn't it?

CHAPTER 16

DO THESE BRITCHES COME IN ANOTHER COLOR?

Ours was the last tour of the day, so Miller and I agreed to hang back and hide when the group returned upstairs. They'd do a roll-call on the coach, so by my estimation we had about ten minutes of hiding before we were hauled out of there.

A scary ten minutes.

A tense ten minutes.

But just ten minutes.

I ducked behind a scene from the French Revolution, coming face to face with a severed head in a basket.

The door to the exhibit closed. I heard a key turn in the lock.

And I waited.

A silence settled over the room. A sudden rumbling startled me. But then I remembered it was a Tube train passing nearby. Silence fell again. An eerie, scary silence.

I imagined the wax figures coming alive then stopped myself. How about if I imagined them dancing together instead? No, because that would still mean them coming alive. How about I just gave my imagination a rest?

I did that instead.

Then, after a while, I whispered, "Hey, Miller? You scared yet?"

There was no reply. I tittered to myself. Browning his britches, I bet.

"Hey…Miller?"

The deal was he'd hide behind a Spanish Inquisition exhibit. I stepped out from behind the French Revolution, took a deep breath, and went over to it.

"Hey, Miller…" I said. I peered behind a man being stretched on a rack.

He wasn't there.

Straightaway I realized what had happened. How could I have been so *dumb*? He'd double-crossed me. He'd promised to hide but joined the group and left.

My imagination woke up. I pictured the group boarding the coach outside Madame Fifi's. I pictured Dwight taking roll-call and Miller saying "Here" at my turn and everyone snickering. And then I pictured the coach leaving. Without me. Miller back at the hotel, failing to alert anybody to the fact that his roomie hadn't turned up…

I dashed to the door. But it was locked.
I began banging on it. A thick, wooden
door like the door to a dungeon.

"HERE!" I shouted.

(A great "Here" it was too. A really
meaty "Here.")

But nobody came. I was locked in. I was
locked in for the night.

CHAPTER 17

I'M NOT ALONE...

"**T**his is all your fault," I told Leo as I looked nervously around at the exhibits. It wasn't really Leo's fault. It was *my* fault. Even so.

My gaze travelled past a man in a mask who held an axe. I looked away then quickly back again to see if he'd moved.

Of course he hadn't moved. None of the waxworks were going to move. They weren't going to move. They weren't going to come alive. And they weren't even going to start dancing. You know why? *Because they were waxworks!* There are only two places waxworks come alive.

One, in movies I'm not old enough to watch yet.

And two, in my imagination.

That's what I told myself. Even as I wandered around looking for another door, feeling like I really needed the bathroom, talking to Leo the Silent as I did so. I told myself, "They're only waxworks—they don't come alive."

Okay, it was time to bring in the big guns. I reached for my phone, ready to dial 911.

(Which would have been the wrong number for emergency services, remember? Told you it would become important.)

But anyway, I had no bars on my phone.

Okay, I thought, *don't panic*. A place like Madame Fifi's was going to have security. A night watchman. And pretty soon that night watchman was going to discover me. Which meant that pretty soon I'd be back with the group. Truckload of trouble etc., but still—a decent mark on the Popularity Score. No face lost.

I listened out for the sound of a security guard. What would a security guard sound like? Shiny black boots on the stone floor. The rattle of keys on a long chain. And whistling—because people in England whistle a lot. They drink tea, eat Marmite, and whistle. It's how they roll.

In the end, I didn't hear him approach at all. Which was probably quite lucky, since I would have jumped out of my skin. Instead what I heard was, "And what might you be doing here?"

Oh, I did—jump out of my skin, I mean. And when I'd returned to my skin I found myself face to face with a very old but kindly looking security guard.

"What's your name?" he asked me with a smile.

I relaxed and told him.

"You're American, are you?"

"Yes, sir."

"Well, I'm pleased to meet you, Rafe," he said. "My name is Albert."

I certainly appreciated his effort to make me feel at ease. He ushered me to the rear of the exhibit, to a door that I hadn't seen when I'd been looking around.

Inside was the night watchman's office. It was a really simple set-up. A desk with what looked like an old newspaper on it. A fire with a pot of water bubbling on it. No kettle for this guy. He was heating his water the American way. Over a stove. Well...a fire.

I took a seat. I was thinking that maybe Albert would pick up the phone to call the Mercury Lodge Hotel. But there was no phone in the office. Matter of fact, Albert didn't have a TV, either. Or even a radio. No wonder he wasn't angry with me: He must have been glad of the company.

"You haven't introduced me to your friend," said Albert.

"Oh," I said. "This is Leo the Silent."

"It's splendid to make your acquaintance, Leo," said Albert.

"Uh...sure..." laughed Leo in reply.

Albert turned to me. "And why, might I ask, are the two of you alone in the Temple of Terrors after hours?"

I took a deep breath and told him.

I guess I did what they call "over-sharing," because I told him pretty much the whole story. Beginning with my lame "Here" at first assembly and ending in the Temple of Terrors.

And I know it's kind of a cliché but it felt good to talk. It felt like I got a lot of stuff off my chest.

"Well, you had better rejoin your group," said Albert. He stood up. He had a weird way of doing things without making much noise. Or even, really, *any* noise. Then he said, "But how would you like your own guided tour of Madame Fifi's first?"

"The whole thing?" I asked. "Not just the Temple of Terrors?"

"The whole thing," said Albert with a smile. "And when it's over, I have a gift for you. Something that might just help you with your bully problem…"

CHAPTER 18

MISSION
ACCOMPLISHED!

Madame Fifi's allows photography, but
that's the problem—everyone, like
everyone, is taking photographs. I'd found
that out earlier when I'd been trying to get
a picture for my Living History trip report
and ended up with some fascinating shots
of the backs of people's heads.

It's not a problem when you have the
place to yourself, though. And even easier
when you have your own tour guide in the
shape of our new friend Albert. He took
Leo and me around the whole place. He
and Leo were getting on like a house on
fire. Leo asked questions while I snapped
away with my camera and scrawled notes
and sketches wherever I could. How cool

was the tour? Put it this way. Before the tour I had nothing for my report. After it, I had enough for two.

It seemed like hours later when we came to the last bit of the tour—a storeroom where the old, unused exhibits were kept. Then Albert gave me my gift— my gift to help beat the bully—and I tucked it in my backpack.

And then, as the battery on my phone ran down to nothing, I managed to get one last picture: It was Albert, standing next to a waxwork of Elizabeth I.

He posed, smiling. Then he indicated to a side door leading onto the street, which hung open.

"And there we have it," he said as he ushered us out. "Dawn is about to break, and I must continue my rounds."

I stepped outside, where the sun was just coming up on a chilly morning. Then turned to him. I wanted to thank him for the gift and for the tour. And to say they were great but...uh, *how do you figure I'm going to get back to the Mercury Lodge when I don't know where the heck I am, don't have any money, and the battery on my phone just died when I took your picture?*

But he wasn't there. And the door had slammed shut. Leaving me standing on the street in the middle of London, in the early morning, without even the taxi fare to the hotel.

Gulp.

"Where to now?" I asked Leo.

A couple of cars passed, but otherwise the street was deserted. And not in a good way. There was a rattle that my imagination insisted was a rat, but it turned out to be a McDonald's carton blowing in the breeze. Even so. It was eerie, being so deserted.

"Back to the river bank?" suggested Leo.

And seeing as that was one of only two places in London I was familiar with, it seemed like the best idea at the time.

I may have been lost but I reckoned I was clever enough to make my way back to the river bank. That much I could manage.

Okay, so the signs to "South Bank" helped.

The point is, I got there. And after worrying it would just be me and a couple of chainsaw-wielding psychopaths, I was pleased to find myself in the company of *other people*. Real people, who weren't waxworks or security guards who pulled confused faces when you said words like "iPod" or "computer." Just your average, normal English early birds: yawning men in suits on their way to work, runners, people beginning to set out stalls...

...and now me.

I don't know if anyone's ever described me as "resourceful," but now was as good a time as any to start. Because right then was when I had my Brilliant Idea. I made my way to the spot where I'd seen the sidewalk artists the day before, whipped out my pencil and sketch pad, and said to the first person who came along, "Caricature, sir?"

CHAPTER 19

IN WHICH I BECOME RICH AND ALMOST FAMOUS

It was thanks to my night at Madame Fifi's that I had the celebrity images fresh in my head.

My first client wanted a caricature of himself with David Beckham, and I was able to oblige. A pretty good likeness of them both, even if I do say so myself. Off went my first satisfied customer.

Along came another. An older lady who wanted herself with Brad Pitt.

Then came a young guy who wanted himself with a soccer player called Wayne Rooney. Someone I hadn't even heard of until a few hours before!

And then, when morning had well and truly broken, and the tourists began to gather, I found myself drawing girls with Justin Bieber and One Direction, guys with Angelina Jolie, middle-aged ladies with Princess Diana. The money was beginning to roll in.

I moved farther along the bank until I came to Waterloo Station, where I packed my things away. I checked my money. By now I had enough for the taxi ride to the Mercury Lodge. But heck, I was having a great time. Why return to the relentless torture of Miller the Killer, the indifference of Jeanne Galletta, and the scorn of everyone else? Not only was I reaping money but also the thanks and praise of my customers.

I was, for perhaps the first time since I'd left Hills Village, having an absolutely brilliant time.

So I took the London Underground. I

went to Piccadilly and saw the sights. Then to Leicester Square, where I set up stall and drew more caricatures. Across the square there were preparations for the night's premiere of the new *Transformers* movie, and I could see camera crews setting up.

Moments later, who should come by but David Beckham.

David Beckham!

He spotted a caricature of himself. There was an awkward moment when I thought he might object to it. But no.

"I *larve* it," he said in his English accent. "Cor blimey, apples and pears, you've done a great job, Rafe. In fact, I larve it so much I'm going to buy it off ya for two thahsand parnds, and give it to my wife Victoriah so she can hang it in our bathroom. 'Cause she likes nothing better than looking at pictures of me when she's on the loo."

(Which is another thing that English people say that's different. They say "on the loo" when they mean "using the bathroom.")

I couldn't take two thousand pounds for the picture. It was far too generous of him. So instead I accepted one thousand, nine hundred and ninety-nine

pounds. And he was so pleased to get a bargain that he invited me to the premiere of the new *Transformers* movie. So along I went, me and Leo on the red carpet. Where I caught the eye of Megan Fox, who's even more gorgeous in the flesh than she is in the movies, if that's possible. And

To Rafe: My Hero! Megan

SMOOCHY SMOOCH

I guess Megan thought I was cute because she insisted on getting our photograph, and...

Oh. It's *that* unbelievable, is it?

MEGAN FOX: FIGMENT OF MY IMAGINATION

Megan Fox was the giveaway, wasn't it? After all, she left the *Transformers* franchise, so what would she be doing at the premiere of the new movie? *Gah!*

Okay, you got me bang to rights. I made some bits up. Yes, the bit about Megan Fox, and the whole *Transformers* routine, and David Beckham and his *two thahsand parnds*. And maybe I kind of exaggerated how popular my caricature service proved to be.

And also how good it was.

But, look, the important thing is that between my (okay, *limited*) artistic abilities and the kind hearts and goodwill of a few English early birds I was able to earn the taxi fare back to the Mercury Lodge. And it was just after 7 a.m. when I eventually arrived.

If I'm honest, I expected to find the place in uproar when I returned. After all, they must have noticed me missing by now. But no. Instead I found the hotel sleepy—more staff around than guests. My absence had gone unnoticed. The truth was, I didn't know whether to be offended or relieved by that.

I crept back up to my room. The room I shared with Miller the Killer. There I found him sleeping soundly. Look at him there. So cute.

I plugged in my phone. Then I went to my backpack and took from it Albert's gift—a wax severed head. I placed it on Miller's pillow, right next to his head. So that this bloody, severed head would be the first thing he saw when he woke up. With the scene set, I took a step back, picked up my phone, aimed it at Miller, and hit "record."

"*MILLER!*" I called.

The bully's eyes sprang open, only to be confronted by the gory head on his pillow.

My phone caught every delicious moment. First Miller squealed like a baby. Then he got himself in a mess trying to escape the head—which ended up rolling into his lap so that for a moment he sat with it between his legs.

Then he tried to push the head off his bed. It developed a life of its own and I got some great footage of him juggling the severed head and whimpering at the same time.

Until, at last, some combination of realizing that (a) I was standing there pointing my phone at him and laughing and (b) the head was a wax head—I mean, even in the grip of shock and terror some tiny bit of Miller's brain must have realized that the wax head felt *wrong* somehow.

And so, eventually, he stopped.

And he looked at me.

He was just about to leap out of bed and give me a beating when I showed him

that with one push of a button I could text
the footage to everyone. Very slowly…
and…patiently…I explained that I was
going to make a deal with him. That the
footage of him screaming like a baby—
not to mention the whimpering—would
never see the light of day as long as he
stopped ragging on me and the rest of
the group.

He agreed, of course. What choice did
he have? (And, yeah, not long after we
arrived back at school, Miller cornered me
in the bathroom after lunch, held my head
over a toilet until I gave him my phone,
and then deleted all the footage.) But the
point is that for the rest of that Living
History trip he was a pussycat. Not a
single cuss escaped his lips, not one
wedgie from his fist, not a flick of his
fingertips. The bullying stopped. All
because of me.

Trouble was, nobody knew I was
responsible.

My good deed went unnoticed.

To make matters worse, I didn't even
benefit from winning William's Wager.

"I'll tell them you spent all night in your bed," sneered Miller that morning. And that was it: any chance of glory dashed.

Just you wait till the journey home, I thought darkly.

You better pray they're not serving spaghetti Bolognese.

CHAPTER 21

P.S.

You know what a P.S. is? It's a postscript. A little bit of extra information when the main show is over. And this here is the postscript to my Living History trip to London.

First, when we'd returned and I wrote up my report, complete with the pictures I'd taken that night, I ended up getting full marks.

[Pause for applause.]

But there was something weird, too. When I went through the pictures—well, you

Rafe's Living History trip to London

100/100 ☆

remember I took one of Albert standing next to Queen Elizabeth I, right before my phone battery died? When I looked at the picture, there was no Albert.

Elizabeth I was there.

But no Albert.

You know what else was weird? When I looked online to see the story of the Madame Fifi haunting, it turned out that the ghost was a Victorian night watchman killed during a freak flood of the basement one night.

A night watchman called Albert.

"Pretty strange, huh?" I said to Leo the Silent. And thinking about it, Leo and Albert had been real friendly that night. They'd got on great.

"Yeah," agreed Leo. "Pretty strange."

Turn the page for an extract
of the top ten bestselling

MIDDLE SCHOOL
THE WORST YEARS OF MY LIFE

TURN 👉

CHAPTER 1

I'M RAFE KHATCHADORIAN, TRAGIC HERO

It feels as honest as the day is *crummy* that I begin this tale of total desperation and woe with me, my pukey sister, Georgia, and Leonardo the Silent sitting like rotting sardines in the back of a Hills Village Police Department cruiser.

Now, there's a pathetic family portrait you don't want to be a part of, believe me. More on the unfortunate Village Police incident later. I need to work myself up to tell you that disaster story.

So anyway, *ta-da*, here it is, book fans, and all of you in need of merit points at school, the true autobio of my life so far. The dreaded middle school years. If you've ever been a middle schooler, you understand already. If you're not in middle school yet, you'll understand soon enough.

But let's face it: Understanding *me*—I mean, *really* understanding me and my nutty life—isn't so easy. That's why it's so hard for me to find people I can trust. The truth is, I don't know who I can trust. So mostly I don't trust anybody. Except my mom, Jules. (Most of the time, anyway.)

So . . . let's see if I can trust you. First, some background.

That's me, by the way, arriving at "prison"—also known as Hills Village Middle School—in Jules's four-by-four. The picture credit goes to Leonardo the Silent.

Getting back to the story, though, I *do* trust one other person. That would actually be Leonardo.

Leo is capital *C* Crazy, and capital *O* Off-the-Wall, but he keeps things real.

Here are some other people I don't trust as far as I can throw a truckload of pianos.

There's Ms. Ruthless Donatello, but you can just call her the Dragon Lady. She teaches English and also handles my favorite subject in sixth grade—after-school detention.

Also, Mrs. Ida Stricker, the vice principal. Ida's pretty much in charge of every breath anybody takes at HVMS.

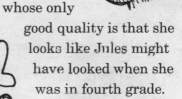

That's Georgia, my super-nosy, super-obnoxious, super-brat sister, whose only good quality is that she looks like Jules might have looked when she was in fourth grade.

There are more on my list, and we'll get to them eventually. Or maybe not. I'm not exactly sure how this is going to work out. As you can probably tell, this is my first full-length book.

But let's stay on the subject of *us* for a little bit. I kind of want to, but how do I know I can trust you with all my embarrassing personal stuff—like the police car disaster story? What are you like? *Inside*, what are you like?

Are you basically a pretty good, pretty decent person? Says who? Says you? Says your 'rents? Says your sibs?

Okay, in the spirit of a possible friendship between us—and this is a huge big deal for me—here's another true confession.

This is what I *actually* looked like when I got to school that first morning of sixth grade.

We still friends, or are you out of here?

Hey—*don't go*—all right? I kind of like you. Seriously. You know how to listen, at least. And believe me, I've got quite the story to tell you.

CHAPTER 2

THE MIDDLE SCHOOL/ MAX SECURITY PRISON

Okay, so imagine the day your great-great-grandmother was born. Got it? Now go back another hundred years or so. And then another hundred. That's about when they built Hills Village Middle School. Of course, I think it was a prison for Pilgrims back then, but not too much has changed. Now it's a prison for sixth, seventh, and eighth graders.

I've seen enough movies that I know when you first get to prison, you basically have two choices: (1) pound the living daylights out of someone so that everyone else will think you're insane and stay out of your way, or (2) keep your head down, try to blend in, and don't get on anyone's bad side.

You've already seen what I look like, so you can probably guess which one I chose. As soon as I got to homeroom, I went straight for the back row and sat as far from the teacher's desk as possible.

There was just one problem with that plan, and his name was Miller. Miller the Killer, to be exact. It's impossible to stay off this kid's bad side, because it's the only one he's got.

But I didn't know any of that yet.

"Sitting in the back, huh?" he said.

"Yeah," I told him.

"Are you one of those troublemakers or something?" he said.

I just shrugged. "I don't know. Not really."

"'Cause this is where all the juvies sit," he said, and took a step closer. "In fact, you're in my seat."

"I don't see your name on it," I told him, and I was just starting to think maybe that was the

wrong thing to say when Miller put one of his
XXXL paws around my neck and
started lifting me like a
hundred-pound dumbbell.

I usually like to keep my head attached to my body, so I went ahead and stood up like he wanted me to.

"Let's try that again," he said. "This is my seat. Understand?"

I understood, all right. I'd been in sixth grade for about four and a half minutes, and I already had a fluorescent orange target on my back. So much for blending in.

And don't get me wrong. I'm not a total wimp. Give me a few more chapters, and I'll show you what I'm capable of. In the meantime, though, I decided to move to some other part of the room. Like maybe somewhere a little less hazardous to my health.

But then, when I went to sit down again, Miller called over. "Uh-uh," he said. "That one's mine too."

Can you see where this is going?

By the time our homeroom teacher, Mr. Rourke, rolled in, I was just standing there wondering what it might be like to spend the next nine months without sitting down.

Rourke looked over the top of his glasses at me. "Excuse me, Mr. Khatch . . . Khatch-a . . . Khatch-a-dor—"

"Khatchadorian," I told him.

"Gesundheit!" someone shouted, and the entire class started laughing.

"Quiet!" Mr. Rourke snapped as he checked his attendance book for my name. "And how are you today, Rafe?" he said, smiling like there were cookies on the way.

"Fine, thanks," I answered.

"Do you find our seating uncomfortable?" he asked me.

"Not exactly," I said, because I couldn't really go into details.

"Then SIT. DOWN. NOW!"

Unlike Miller the Killer, Mr. Rourke definitely has two sides, and I'd already met both of them.

Since nobody else was stupid enough to sit right in front of Miller, that was the only seat left in the room.

And because I'm the world's biggest idiot sometimes, I didn't look back when I went to sit in my chair. Which is why I hit the dirt as I went down — all the way down — to the floor.

The good news? Given the way things had started off, I figured middle school could only get better from here.

The bad news? I was wrong about the good news.

If you enjoyed reading

MIDDLE SCHOOL

HOW I GOT LOST IN LONDON

why not catch up on the rest of Rafe's hilarious adventures in the four other bestselling books in the **Middle School series**

Look out for the two new
adventures to come in 2014,
Middle School: Ultimate Showdown
and **Middle School: Save Rafe!**

JAMES PATTERSON
GETS KIDS READING

www.jamespatterson.co.uk

WORLD BOOK DAY *fest*

6 MARCH 2014

Want to **READ** more?

 your **LOCAL BOOKSHOP**

- Get some great recommendations for what to read next

- Meet your favourite authors & illustrators at brilliant events

- Discover books you never even knew existed!

 your **LOCAL LIBRARY**

You can browse and borrow from a HUGE selection of books and get recommendations of what to read next from expert librarians—all for FREE! You can also discover libraries' wonderful children's and family reading activities.

 WWW.BOOKSELLERS.ORG.UK/ BOOKSHOPSEARCH

 WWW.FINDALIBRARY.CO.UK

 Visit **WWW.WORLDBOOKDAY.COM** to discover a whole *new* world of books!

- Downloads and activities
- Cool games, trailers and videos
- Author events in your area
- News, competitions and new books —all in a **FREE** monthly email

AND MORE!